Text copyright © 2012 Niki Massse Schoenfeldt, Illustrations copyright © 2012 John Wes Thomas

Inquiries should be addressed to: Shenanigan Books, 84 River Road, Summit New Jersey, 07901.

Library of Congress Control Number: 2012936165

ISBN: 978-1-934860-13-7

Printed in China
first edition 1 2012
This product conforms to CPSIA 2008

Shenanigan Books

Don't Let the Bedbugs Bite!

Niki Masse Schoenfeldt
Pictures by John Wes Thomas

One wintry eve, I lay in bed,
Listening to what my mama said.
She tucked me in that cold, cold night
And said "Don't let the bedbugs bite."

"Bedbugs!" I shrieked, "Now what are those?
Some nasty creatures who'll eat my toes?"
"Relax," she said, "no need to fear.
We don't have any bedbugs here..."

"It's just a saying from olden days,
A simple, silly goodnight phrase."
Then she smiled and left the room,
And left me staring in the gloom.

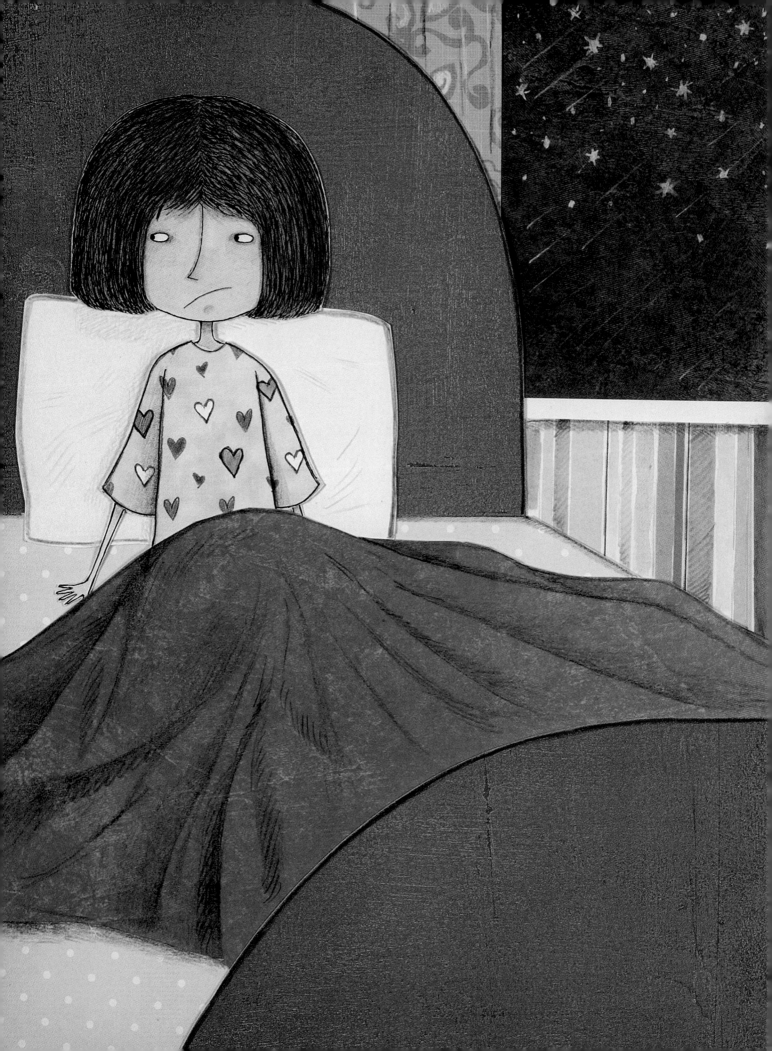

When suddenly out of the blue,
A tiny voice called out, "Hey you!"
I looked around, saw nothing there,
But then that nothing pulled my hair.

"Ouch!" I cried. It tugged once more.
I pulled away...fell to the floor!
Be brave, I thought, don't be weak,
It won't hurt to take a peek.

I stared across my empty bed
And rubbed my eyes when something said,
"Don't come closer!" came the voice.
But I did. I had no choice.

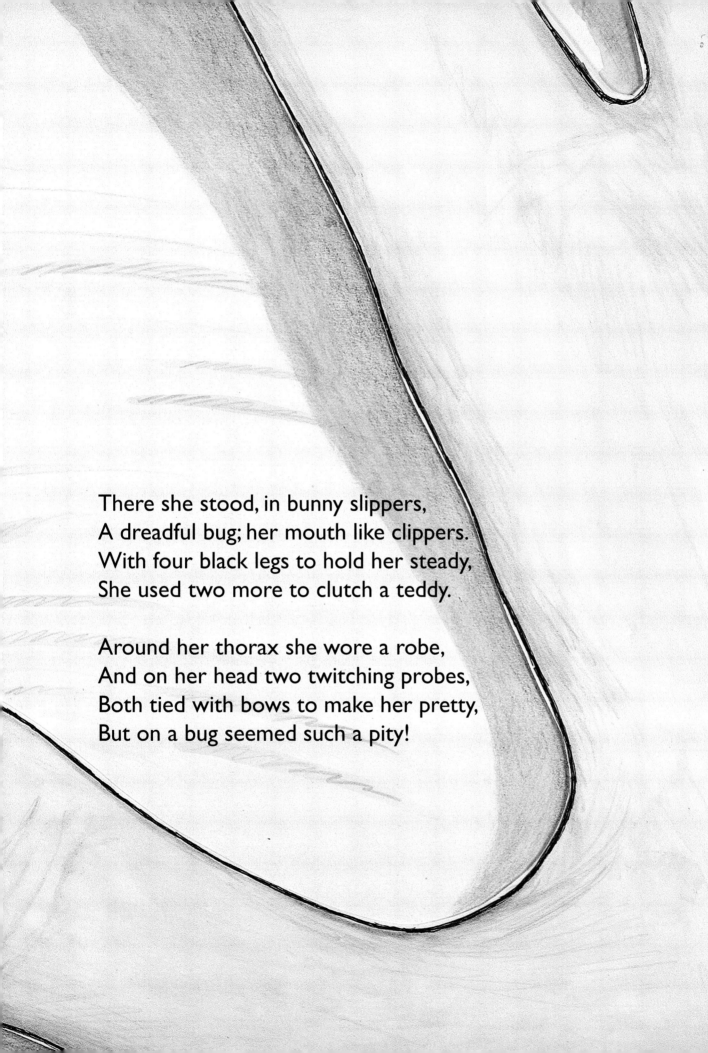

There she stood, in bunny slippers,
A dreadful bug; her mouth like clippers.
With four black legs to hold her steady,
She used two more to clutch a teddy.

Around her thorax she wore a robe,
And on her head two twitching probes,
Both tied with bows to make her pretty,
But on a bug seemed such a pity!

She stood her ground, but shook with fright.
"So you're a human. Do you bite?"
"Who me?" I asked. "Oh you're confused.
'Cause you're the biter," I accused.

I found the bug spray, aimed the can,
"My mom is right," the bug began.
"She says it is so very sad
That humans think all bugs are bad."

"But bedbugs bite us in our sleep!
You're not the kind of friend I keep."
"You're wrong!" she said, "I'm not a thug.
I'm just a sleepy ladybug."

"A ladybug!" I said surprised
'Cause in that robe she was disguised.
"You're not allowed inside my house
No more than if… you were a mouse!"

"It's cold outside," she said to me,
"Inside is where I want to be.
I eat aphids and you're not one
My hibernating time has come."

"You want to sleep here in my bed?"
"Why not?" the little bugling said.
"I won't bite, I'm beneficial...
Ask any mom or bug official."

And then that bug didn't look so scary.
She wasn't mean, she was just wary.
She couldn't live in snow and ice.
She didn't need to ask me twice.

And so I let her crawl back in
Under the covers where she had been.
I tucked her in, turned off the light
and said, "Don't let the bedbugs bite!"

For Mudskippers Critique Group
who took a look at a poem I didn't know what to do with and yelled, "picture book!" -
You gals were right. Also in memory of my memere, Yvonne Dextrader, who instilled in
me her distaste for pesky bugs and her love of Lady Bugs which she believed brought
good luck. - She was right.
– Niki Masse Schoenfeldt

For Henry
– John Wes Thomas